Do I Have to Wear a Coat?

A journey through the seasons

RACHEL ISADORA

Nancy Paulsen Books

To Roger, Elodie, and Jack . . .
who never want to wear their coats

NANCY PAULSEN BOOKS
An imprint of Penguin Random House LLC, New York

Copyright © 2020 by Rachel Isadora
Penguin supports copyright. Copyright fuels creativity, encourages diverse voices, promotes free speech, and creates a vibrant culture. Thank you for buying an authorized edition of this book and for complying with copyright laws by not reproducing, scanning, or distributing any part of it in any form without permission. You are supporting writers and allowing Penguin to continue to publish books for every reader.

Nancy Paulsen Books is a trademark of Penguin Random House LLC.

Visit us online at penguinrandomhouse.com

Library of Congress Cataloging-in-Publication Data is available.
Manufactured in China by RR Donnelley Asia Printing Solutions Ltd.
ISBN 9780525516606
3 5 7 9 10 8 6 4 2

Design by Marikka Tamura
Text set in Archer
The art was done in ink and watercolor.

On a
rainy **SPRING** day,

on a
hot **SUMMER** day,

on a
chilly **FALL** day,

on a
cold **WINTER** day ...

Do I have to wear a coat?

I Love SPRING

THE 4 SEASONS: **SPRING** • SUMMER • FALL • WINTER

Spring is for playing outside!

Yay! No more coats.

And smelling the flowers.

These are for Grandma.

On rainy days, we put on raincoats and rain boots.

After the rain,
we get mud and worms.

THE 4 SEASONS: **SPRING** • SUMMER • FALL • WINTER

In spring, we say hello to new farm babies.

Nice wool coat!

Such a cute piglet!

And we watch ducklings waddle in a row.

We play baseball in the park.

Go, team!

We draw on the sidewalk.

THE 4 SEASONS: **SPRING** • SUMMER • FALL • WINTER

We hop and skip.

I love hopscotch!

We ride our bikes everywhere.

The sun is warm and sweet berries grow.

I eat one.
I pick one.
I eat one.

Save some for Mommy.

Everyone loves picnics.

Even the ants!

I Love SUMMER

Summer is for cool treats.

We love ice cream

and watermelon

and getting sticky.

THE 4 SEASONS: SPRING • SUMMER • FALL • WINTER

In summer, bees buzz.

I'm not gonna move!

We blow bubbles.

And fireflies light up the sky.

We are busy morning, noon, and night.

Swinging rackets.

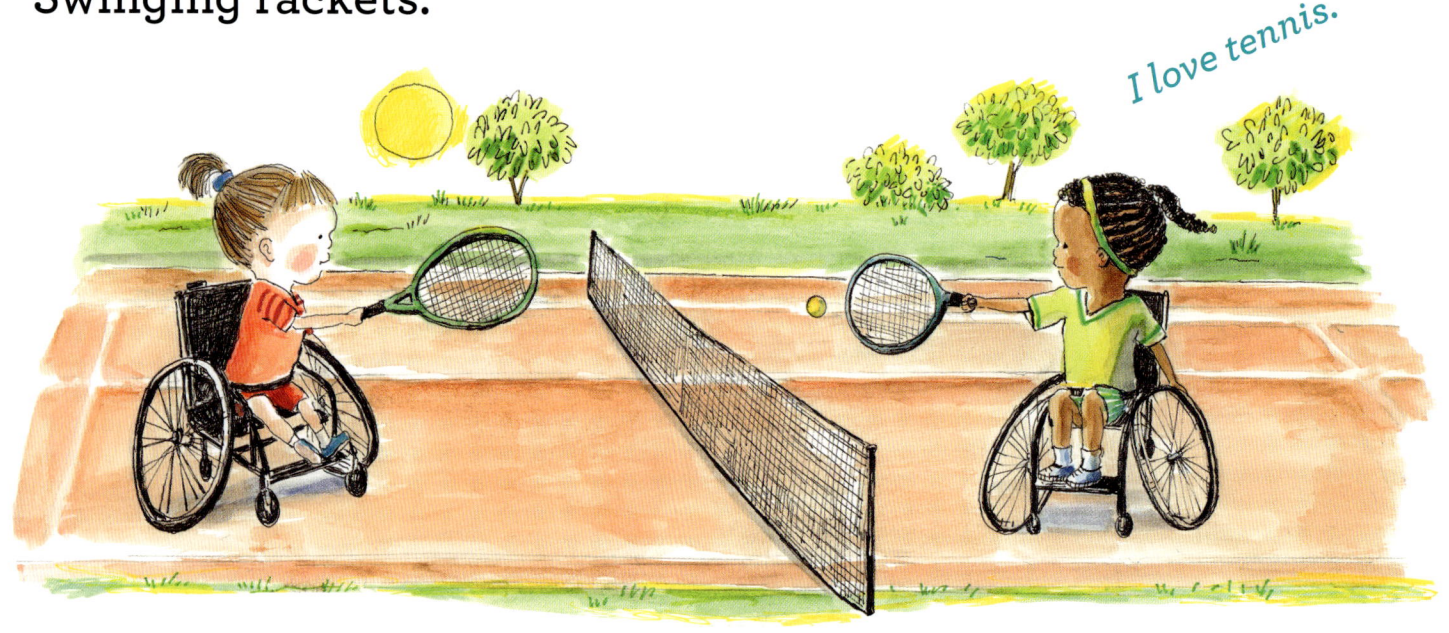

I love tennis.

Flying kites.

It's almost as high as the plane!

THE 4 SEASONS: SPRING • **SUMMER** • FALL • WINTER

Huddling around the campfire on chilly nights.

Let's tell scary stories!

When it is hot, we cool off at the beach.

I have to wear water wings— but you don't!

We eat lunch on the sand.

Seagulls like peanut butter too!

Summer is full of surprises!

If we're lucky, we find four-leaf clovers.

And sometimes we see a rainbow!

I Love **FALL**

Fall is for meeting our teacher—and making new friends.

I like your backpack.

I got new shoes.

For apple picking.

Uh-oh!

THE 4 SEASONS: SPRING • SUMMER • **FALL** • WINTER

And soccer games.

On cool days, we wear warm sweaters.

Looking good, Henry!

The trees lose their leaves.

THE 4 SEASONS: SPRING • SUMMER • **FALL** • WINTER

And we dive into them!

Did we lose Henry?

Fall is for hayrides,

pumpkins,

Who's your dentist?

and trick-or-treating.

I'll put on my coat later.

THE 4 SEASONS: SPRING • SUMMER • FALL • WINTER

The days get colder and the birds fly south.

Bye-bye, birdies.

I Love WINTER

THE 4 SEASONS: SPRING • SUMMER • FALL • **WINTER**

Winter is the time to bundle up.

You have to wear a coat!

Or to get cozy inside.

Sometimes it snows all night—

Wow! It's beautiful!

and we get to play all day . . .

building snowmen,

You need a scarf!

THE 4 SEASONS: SPRING • SUMMER • FALL • **WINTER**

throwing snowballs,

Watch out!

and making snow angels.

We skate on the ice.

Too slippery!

We breathe frosty air.

THE 4 SEASONS: SPRING • SUMMER • FALL • **WINTER**

Winter is for mugs of hot chocolate.

Cuddling up with a book

He looks like you!

and each other.

In **SPRING**
I wore a raincoat.

In **SUMMER**
it was too hot for a coat.

In **FALL**
we wore sweaters.

In **WINTER**
I *HAD* to wear a coat!

Did you have to wear a coat?